Center for Responsive Schools, Inc., is a not-for-profit educational organization.

© 2023 by Fly Five: The Social and Emotional Learning Curriculum

All rights reserved. No part of this book may be reproduced in any form or by any electronic or mechanical means, including information storage and retrieval systems, without permission in writing from the publisher, except by a reviewer, who may quote brief passages in a review.

First edition, April 2023
10 9 8 7 6 5 4 3 2 1

This book is part of the Adventures of the Center City Kids series.

Fly Five Team:
Jazmine Franklin, Chief Program Officer
Anjail Kenyatta, Director of Content and Curriculum Development
Samantha Nacht, Creative and Art Director
Ellie Cornecelli, Director of Professional Development and Engagement
Janessa Martin, Curriculum and Instructional Designer
Najah Hijazi, Curriculum and Instructional Designer
Angelica Williams, Digital and Graphic Designer
Clay Caricofe, Graphic Designer
Josh Frederick, Graphic Designer
Negene Cord-Cruz, Graphic Designer
Hannah Shearer, Graphic Design Specialist

Contributing Writers: Rebecca Crutchfield, Savannah Elliott, Anjail Kenyatta, Amy Martin, Janessa Martin, Amanda Millard

Contributing Illustrators: Christina Dill, Samantha Jo, Kenny Kiernan, Lauren Scott, Kaitlyn Terrey, Ernon Wright

Concept Illustrator: Monika Suska

ISBN: 978-1-950317-36-3
Library of Congress Control Number: 2023931569
Printed in China

Avenue A Books
An imprint of
Fly Five: The Social and Emotional Learning Curriculum
85 Avenue A, P.O. Box 718
Turners Falls, MA 01376-0718
800-360-6332
flyfivesel.org

This book is dedicated to all of the students
who follow the classroom rules—
and take care of their community!

"Attention, Students! Attention!"

announced Principal Agnew over the intercom.

"Today Coach Khan is out. PE will be held in your classrooms. Thank you."

NOOOOOOO,

thought Kofi. He wanted to show off his new soccer kick.

"**Awwwwww,**" whined Luna. She wanted to play that *rainbow-colored* parachute game.

"*Who's going to teach PE?*" asked a concerned Imani.

"Settle down, class," said Mrs. Tuttle. "I'm sure that there will be a wonderful substitute today. And they will be just as fun and kind as Coach Khan."

Shen and Blake weren't so sure about that.

Looking at their worried faces,
Mrs. Tuttle continued,
"Room 103, I know you can meet this change
with positivity and patience."

TAP! TAP! TAP! TAP!

Then at 11:05 am on the dot,
there was a knock on the door.

All the students in Room 103 held their breath.

In walked the substitute. He was tall. He carried a basketball under his arm. And he was dressed in all red, from his shirt down to his sneakers.

The students of Room 103 sat quietly and stared.

He thundered,

"My name is Mr. Whirley.

And I'm the PE teacher for today!"

"Well, nice to meet you, Mr. Whirley,"
Mrs. Tuttle responded with a smile.

Before Mrs. Tuttle walked out the door,
she pointed to the board.
"Room 103, be on your best behavior.
And don't forget our special classroom rules
and responsibilities for PE today," she said.

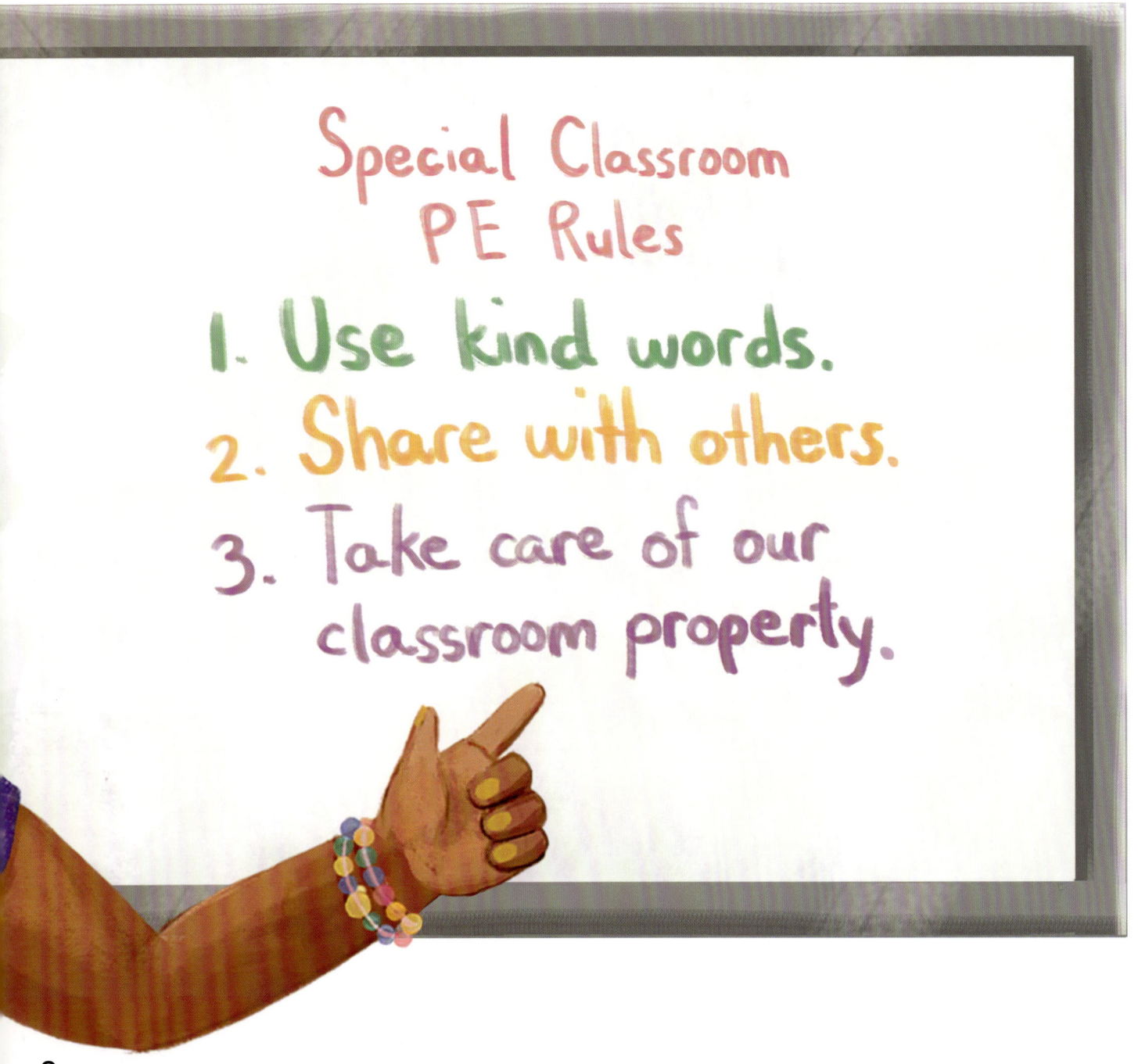

Mr. Whirley stood in front of the students. He slammed his hand on the table and announced, "RULES SCHMULES! You kids look like you behave well enough!"

Kofi leaned toward Luna.
"What are 'schmules'?" he whispered.
"I don't know," she answered.

"Let's go ahead and get a game started. Everyone, sit on your desk. It's time for Garbage Can Basketball!"

Everyone cheered!

They had played this game before.

"Mr. Whirley!" shouted Gabriel. "Wait, we need to put stuff away that might break!"

"Yeah!" added Anisa pointing to Mrs. Tuttle's list of rules. "Take care of classroom property!"

"The classroom belongs to all of us," added Gabriel. "We have to take care of it!" he said.

"RULES SCHMULES!"

Mr. Whirley said again.
"Let's have fun!"

"PLAY

BALL"

Shen grabbed the ball first.
But instead of passing it to a classmate,
he put it on his finger and tried to spin it.

"Hey, Shen! That's not fair!" said Gabriel.

"But it's fun," answered Shen, "and that's the only rule today!"

"No! You have to share!" complained Imani. "It's what we always do!"

"I guess so," mumbled Shen. He passed the ball to Jade.

But Jade dropped it.

"That's lazy, Jade!"
Blake yelled out.

"Hey, use kind words!"
Luna said.

"I was only kidding," mumbled Blake.

Jade felt hurt and frustrated. She picked up the ball and threw it hard.

BONK!

The ball bounced off of a table.

Then it flew toward Mrs. Tuttle's desk. Everyone gasped!

THUD!

The ball hit her favorite mug.

It landed on the floor but didn't break.
All the students exhaled.

The ball continued to bounce around the tables.
It just couldn't be caught.

BOINK!

It slipped out of Doba's hands and bounced off Kofi's shoulder.

BOING!

It flew over Luna's head.

And it hit a basket of books.

"I told you we should have put stuff away!" Gabriel exclaimed.

Each time the ball bounced, Mr. Whirley ran with his arms outstretched.

His legs moved so quickly!

They looked like spinning bicycle tires turning this way and that.

Then, the ball made one final dangerous turn.
It was headed right toward Goldie, the class fish!

Mr. Whirley's eyes grew big like two chocolate donuts. He lunged forward, knocking pencils off every desk in his path.

All of the students in Room 103 held their breath.

Mr. Whirley whizzed through the air like a rocket. He caught the ball right before it hit the fishbowl. The students of Room 103 stood up and cheered!

"Mr. Whirley, you saved our fish!" exclaimed Shen.

"Yeah," said Luna, "but our classroom is a mess!"

"Hmmmm . . . Maybe we should take a look at those rules you keep talking about." Mr. Whirley read them aloud:

"1. Use kind words.

2. Share with others.

3. Take care of our classroom property."

"Do you all really do these things?" he asked.

"YES!" the class chanted together.

"THE CLASSROOM BELONGS TO ALL OF US."

"Don't worry, Mr. Whirley. We know what to do," said Imani.

Mr. Whirley watched as the students scurried around like busy bees in a beehive.

Jade and Anisa straightened up Mrs. Tuttle's desk.

Kofi and Luna organized the fallen books.

Gabriel and Imani put all the pencils back on the tables.

Shen and Doba put all the pieces of paper in a nice neat stack.

And Blake checked on Goldie the class fish just to make sure it was okay.

"Are you okay, Goldie?"

Suddenly, they heard a soft tap on the door. In walked Mrs. Tuttle!

She looked around the room and smiled happily at her class. "How did everything go, Mr. Whirley?" she asked.

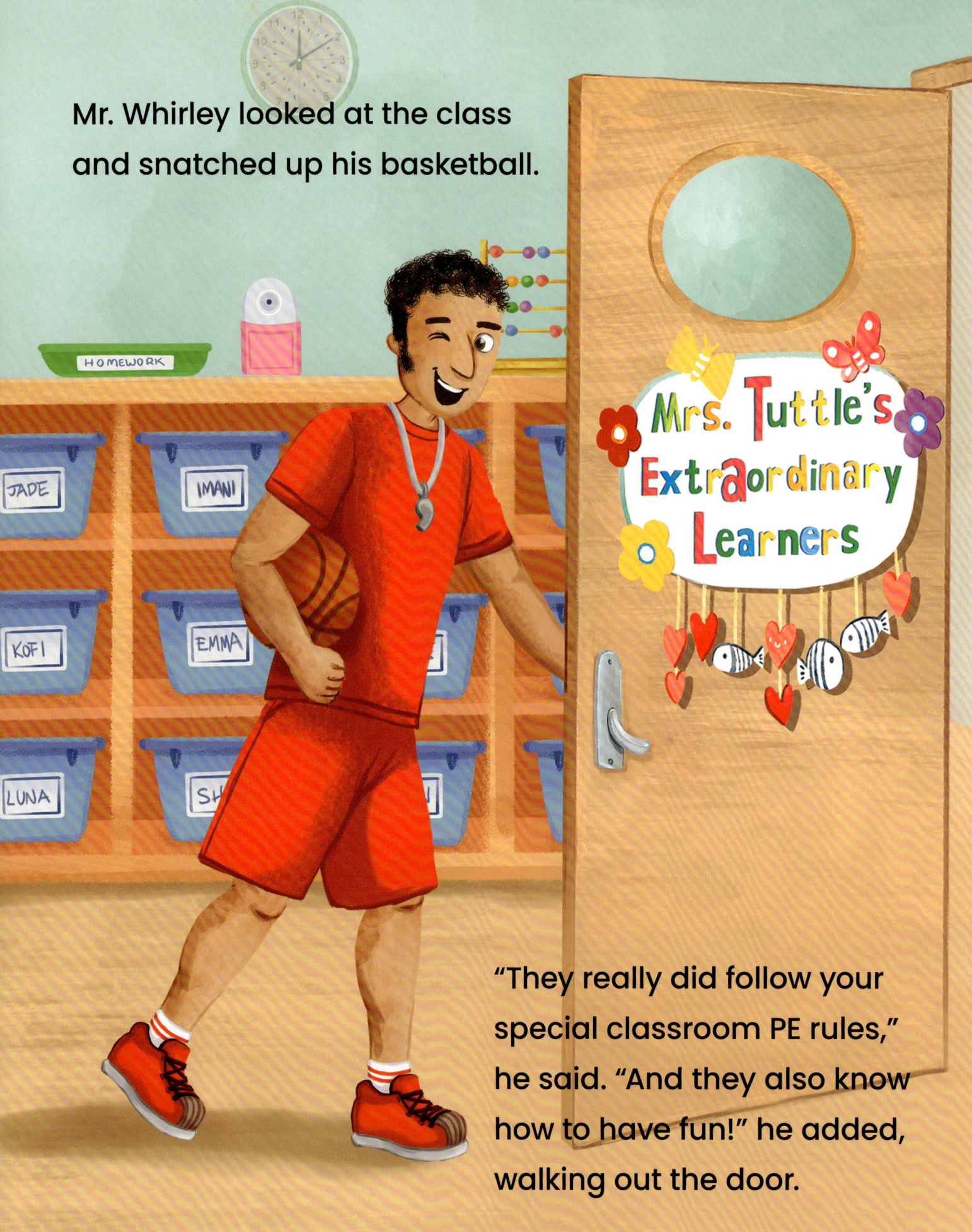

Mr. Whirley looked at the class and snatched up his basketball.

"They really did follow your special classroom PE rules," he said. "And they also know how to have fun!" he added, walking out the door.

"Mrs. Tuttle!" "Guess what?!"

"You won't believe this!"

Room 103 began talking all at once.
Each person wanted to be heard.
They had so much to tell Mrs. Tuttle.

Mrs. Tuttle called out, "Settle down, class.
As soon as we come back from lunch,
you all can tell me all about PE and Mr. Whirley."

"Wow!" "No way!"

"Listen!"

As the class made their way toward the cafeteria, Anisa saw something out of the corner of her eye. It was none other than Mr. Whirley . . .

. . . whirling into Room 105!

Adventures of the Center City Kids

Adventures of the Center City Kids is a collection of engaging, relevant, and relatable books for children and youth that promote literacy skills, celebrate family, and amplify cultural diversity. This series supports academic, social, and emotional growth in five core competencies: cooperation, assertiveness, responsibility, empathy, and self-control. The Adventures of the Center City Kids series inspires readers to create a good life for themselves, their families, and their community.

Cooperation

An engaging book series about the ability to establish and maintain new relationships, resolve conflicts, and be a contributing member of the classroom and community.

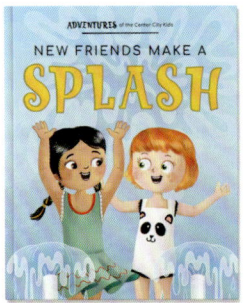  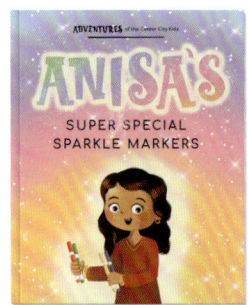 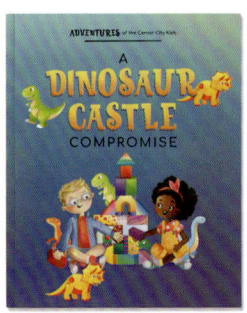

Assertiveness

An engaging book series about how to stand up for one's ideas without hurting or negating others, how to seek help, and how to persevere with a challenging task.

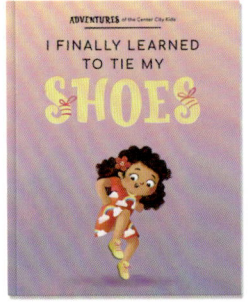 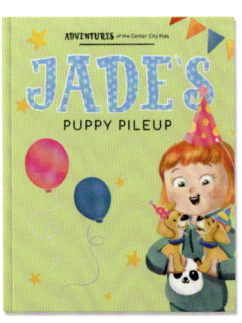 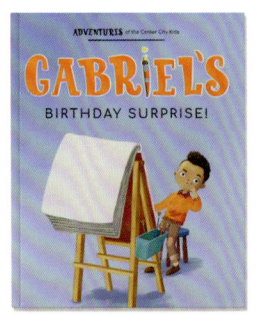 

Order the entire collection at flyfivesel.org

Responsibility

An engaging book series about the ability to motivate oneself to act and follow through on expectations and the ability to define a problem, consider the consequences, and choose a positive solution.

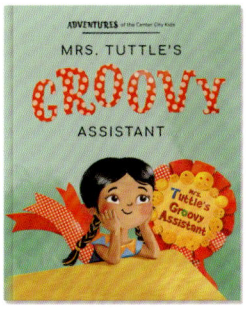 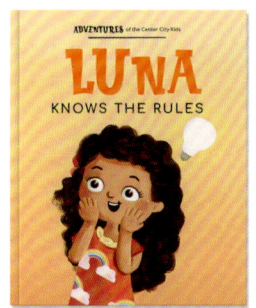 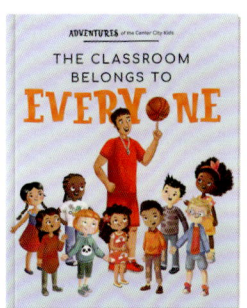 

Empathy

An engaging book series about the ability to recognize one's emotions and be receptive to new ideas and perspectives.

 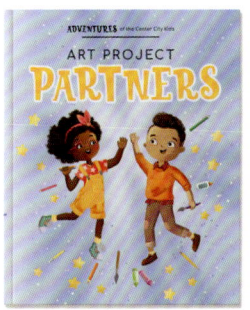 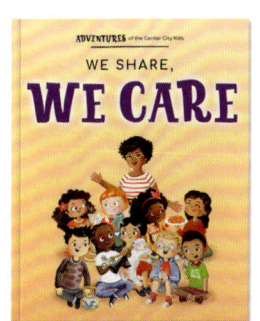 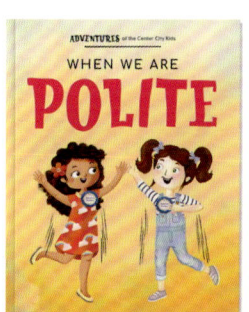

Self-Control

An engaging book series about the ability to recognize and regulate one's thoughts, emotions, and behaviors in order to be successful in the moment and remain on a successful trajectory.

 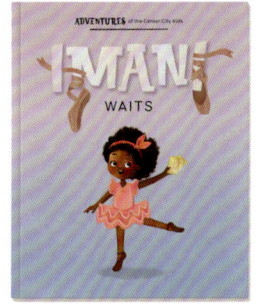 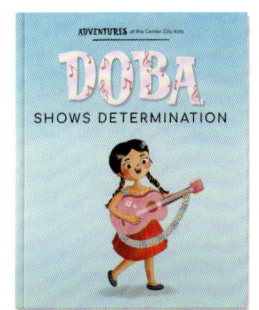 

CENTER CITY

1. Using the map, where do you think Mr. Whirley lives? Explain.

2. What do you think is Mr. Whirley's favorite place to visit?

3. Where would Mr. Whirley take the class on a field trip? Explain.